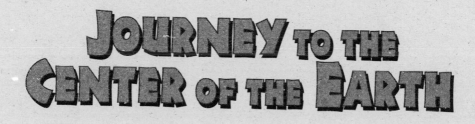

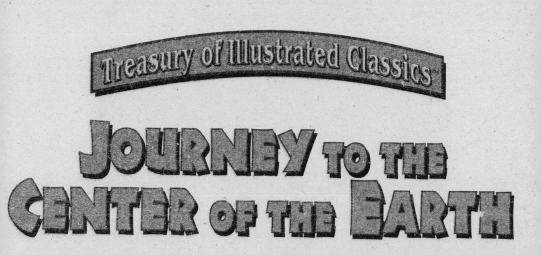

Treasury of Illustrated Classics

Journey to the Center of the Earth

by
Jules Verne

Adapted by
Kathleen Rizzi

Illustrated by
Pulsar Studio

Modern Publishing
A Division of Unisystems, Inc.
New York, New York 10022

Series UPC: 39305

Cover art by Pete Roberts

Contents

CHAPTER 1
A Remarkable Discovery

I can remember the adventure as clearly as if it happened yesterday. It began on the 24th of May, 1863. My uncle, Professor Liedenbrock, rushed into his little house on Konigstrasse, one of the oldest streets in the oldest section of the city of Hamburg. He startled me and Martha, the housekeeper.

On the way, he threw down his walking stick and hat and shouted, "Alex, come at once!" Before I even had time to get to my feet, he shouted again. I rushed toward his study.

Although Otto Liedenbrock was a good-hearted man, he was stern and made most people anxious. He was a mineralogy professor at the university in Hamburg. He was in awe of his own mind and abilities. He was known to be quite a scholar in his field.

He had the genius of a true geologist. He could easily name and identify each of the elements known to man by their shape and appearance. The Liedenbrock name was respected in colleges worldwide for his many discoveries. The leaders in his field often sought his advice.

His goddaughter Gretchen, who was eighteen years old, Martha, and I lived with him. As his nephew and an orphan, I was my uncle's laboratory assistant. I enjoyed the job since I liked geology and all related sciences.

One could live happily enough in this little old house in spite of the restless impatience of its master. As excitable as he was, my uncle was very fond of me. But at this moment, this tall gentleman, who looked ten years younger than his fifty years, was shouting for my attention.

I reminded myself that there was no better way to deal with such impatience than swift obedience. So I rushed into his study at once.

The study was like a museum, with every specimen in place and labeled. How often I could recall staying in his study to catalog the samples instead of going out to play with my friends. As I entered his study now, I saw my uncle sitting on a velvet chair holding a book that had his full attention.

"Look at this remarkable book!" he said. The book was faded and falling apart. "This is the Heims Kringla of Snorre Turlleson, the most famous Icelandic author of the twelfth century! It is the chronicle of the Norwegian princes who ruled in Iceland. It is in the original Icelandic!"

"Oh," I said, without interest. "Is the type good?"

"Type! This is not a printed book, you fool! This is a runic manuscript!"

"Runic?" I asked.

"Runic characters were used in Iceland in the past," my uncle explained.

I was just about to look at this wonderful book when a dirty piece of parchment slipped out of it and fell on the floor.

"What's this?" my uncle cried, leaping to pick up the piece of paper. "These are runic letters. They are exactly like those in Snorre Turlleson's manuscript. But, what is their meaning?"

He continued: "There is a secret in this message, Alex. I will discover the key. "Sit there and write."

I took a seat immediately and wrote as he directed. I did my best to write every letter of our alphabet that corresponded with each of the Icelandic characters. This was the result:

mm.rnlls esrevel seeclde
sgtssmf vnteief niedrke
kt,samn atrateS saodrrn
emtnael nvaect rrilSa
Atsaar .nvcrc ieaabs
ccrmi eevtVl frAntv
dt,iac oseibo Kediil

"This is a cryptogram, or puzzle," he said. "The letters are purposely mixed up. There may be some great discovery concealed here!"

Then my uncle carefully compared the book and the parchment. "These two writings were done by different people," he said. "The puzzle was done after the book. I know, since the first letter is a double m, a letter that is not to be found in Turlleson's book. It was only added to the alphabet in the fourteenth century. There are two hundred years between the manuscript and the document."

I had to admit that this was a logical conclusion.

"I imagine," continued my uncle, "that the owner of this book wrote these mysterious letters. But who was the owner? Can we find his name in the manuscript?"

My uncle carefully examined the blank pages of the book. On the second page, he noticed a sort of stain. It looked like an ink blot.

He thought that he could see some half-obliterated letters. With the help of his microscope, he was able to read them.

"Arne Saknussemm!" he cried happily. "That is the name of another Icelander, a genius of the sixteenth century, a celebrated alchemist! Perhaps Saknussemm hid news of some surprising invention in the puzzle? It must be so!"

My uncle's imagination took off at this thought. "Neither of us will eat or sleep until I get to the secret of this document."

"Oh!" I sighed at his latest plan.

"Saknussemm was a very well informed man but since he was not writing in his own mother tongue," my uncle continued, "he probably used Latin. But it is Latin in disorder. Let's write the words vertically

instead of horizontally. This might help us unscramble everything."

"Yes," I said absentmindedly. My attention was now on a portrait of Gretchen. I loved her with all of my heart, a fact my uncle was not yet aware of.

I did as he suggested and wrote the letters.

```
l y l o a t
l o l w r c
o u , n G h
v w m d r e
e e y e e n t e
```

"Good," said my uncle, without reading them. "Now write those words in a horizontal line."

I obeyed. This was the result:

Iyloat lolwre ou,nGh vwmdre eeyeente

"Excellent!" my uncle said, taking the paper out of my hands. "This is beginning to look just like an ancient document. The vowels and the consonants are grouped together in equal disorder. There are even

capital letters in the middle of words, just as in Saknussemm's parchment."

I considered these remarks very clever.

"Now," said my uncle, "I'll read the sentence. I think I have figured out a method for deciphering the code."

And my uncle, to his great astonishment, read, "I love you well, my own dear Gretchen!"

"What's this?" cried my uncle. "Aha! You are in love with Gretchen!"

"Yes! No!" I stammered.

"You love Gretchen," he said dreamily. "Well, let us apply the process I have suggested to the document in question." He left the discussion of Gretchen for another time.

Applying the formula, he dictated the following:

mmessvnkaSenrA.icefdoK.segni
tamvrtnecertserrette,rotaisadva,ed
necsedsadnelacartniiilvIsiratracSarb
mvtabiledmekmeretarcsilvcolsleffe
nSnI.

"That's not it," cried my uncle, pounding his hand on the desk. "There's no sense in it." He darted out and down the stairs. He rushed out the door and disappeared down the street.

I wanted to tell Gretchen all about all that had happened, but I didn't dare leave the house in case my uncle returned and needed me. So I began to catalog a new collection of rocks that we had just received. But this work did not keep me from thinking about that old document.

I could not decipher it. I fanned myself with the bit of paper. As I did, I caught sight of the Latin words "craterem," "terrestre," and others. These hints gave me the first glimpse of the truth. I had discovered the key to the puzzle!

I was filled with terror and overwhelmed. Could what I read really have been done? A mortal man was able to penetrate–!

"No! It can't be," I declared. "I can't let

him read this!" I was about to fling it into the fire to destroy this secret. But the study door opened, and my uncle appeared. I put the document back on the table just in time.

My uncle sat in his armchair, pen in hand, and began to try to solve the puzzle. He worked all night long. When I awoke next morning, that tireless worker was still at his post.

I resolved to tell him nothing, because

if he knew, nothing on earth could stop him. He would risk his life and stop at nothing to do what other geologists have never been able to achieve.

But in the end, I changed my mind. My hunger overcame me and I could wait no longer for a meal. My uncle was determined to fast until he achieved his purpose.

"Uncle," I said,

"Yes," he replied, as if just waking

from a dream.

"The key to the document . . ." I began, sighing.

My uncle stared intensely at me over his spectacles. "What exactly is it that you are trying to say?" he asked.

"There, read that!" I said, giving him the paper on which I had written. "Read it backward."

I had barely finished my sentence when my uncle broke out into a cry of joy. "Aha, clever Saknussemm!" he cried. He read the whole document from the last letter to the first.

When translated, this is what was written:

"Descend, bold traveler, into the crater of the jokul of Sneffels, which the shadow of Scartaris touches before the kalends of July, and you will attain the center of the earth; which I have done, Arne Saknussemm."

My uncle was joyous. He could not believe what he had read. He wanted to immediately spring into action. "We will pack after dinner," he said.

CHAPTER 2
Talk of a Journey Never Before Undertaken

I was frozen in place. Professor Liedenbrock was determined to make a journey to the center of the earth. I thought it was nonsense!

"Alex," he said, "I could not have done this without you. Rest assured that you will share in the glory of this discovery. But we must keep it a secret."

"Do you really think anyone would take this seriously?" I asked.

"Of course. Any geologist would rush to follow the footsteps of Saknussemm," he replied.

"But we have no proof that this document is real," I said.

"That is what we shall see. What are

your concerns? Speak as a colleague, not as a nephew."

I asked him to explain the words "Jokul", "Sneffel", and "Scartaris", which I had never heard. He referred to a map. My uncle pointed to volcanoes, which are called jokuls in Iceland. Near Reykjavik, there was a mountain named Snaefell.

"It is five thousand feet high. Its crater leads down to the center of the earth!" he exclaimed.

"But that is impossible," I said.

"Why?" asked my uncle severely.

"Because this crater is evidently filled with lava and burning rocks, and therefore—"

"There has been only one eruption—in 1219. It is no longer considered an active volcano," he said.

I could hardly argue with him. "What is the meaning of Scartaris, and what have the kalends of July to do with it?" I asked.

My uncle said the kalends of July were the last few days in June. During that time the shadow cast by one of the peaks of Scartaris would fall onto the crater that led to the center of the earth, according to Saknussemm's message.

"Well, then," I said, "I am forced to admit that Saknussemm's sentence is clear. But as for reaching the center of the earth, he did not achieve it. I do not believe that he ever made the journey and returned."

"What's your reason?" asked my uncle.

"It would be impossible to make such a journey, due to the intense heat at the earth's center and the pressure one would encounter traveling to it," I said.

"No one knows for sure what is going on in the interior of this globe. Science is not perfect. Every new theory is soon replaced by a newer one," he said. "We will now have an opportunity to discover the truth or fiction of these theories!"

I was beginning to see his position.

"You see," he added, "there is no proof at all of this internal heat. My opinion is that there is no such thing. Besides, we shall see for ourselves."

"Very well, we shall see," I replied, feeling myself carried off by his enthusiasm. "That is, if it is possible to see anything at all."

"Can't we depend upon electric light? May we not even expect light from the atmosphere?"

"Yes," I said, "that is possible, too."

"It most certainly will be true," exclaimed my uncle triumphantly. "But, don't say a word about the whole business. No one should discover the center of the earth before we do!"

After this, I had to get some fresh air. I walked without direction but soon found I was on the road to Altona. On my way, I bumped into Gretchen, who was already on her way home. I told her of all that had happened. We walked on silently for some time.

When we returned home I expected to find my uncle asleep. But instead he was shouting and ordering porters and messengers about.

"Alex! Your boxes are not packed. We must prepare," he bellowed.

"Are we really going?" I asked in shock.

"Of course. What have you been wasting your time doing?" he asked. "We leave the day after tomorrow."

I couldn't believe it. I went into my room and closed the door. My uncle had spent the day making travel arrangements and purchasing the tools and apparatuses we needed for this trip. The hallway of the house was cluttered with rope ladders, knotted cords, torches, flasks, grappling irons, pickaxes, and iron shod sticks.

It was a long, awful night. The next morning, although I didn't want to face it, Gretchen's sweet voice called at my door.

"My dear Alex," she said as I came out of my room. "Are you feeling better? I spoke with Uncle Otto about all of his plans. He will no doubt succeed. You will participate in the greatest scientific journey ever undertaken. When you return you will be his equal and highly regarded," she said as her cheeks blushed.

We went into my uncle's study. In spite of my attempts to discourage him, he said we would leave at once. He wanted to arrive in time to see the shadow of Scartaris touch the crater of Snaefell.

At half-past five in the morning, there was a rattle of wheels outside. A large carriage was there to take us to the railway station. It was soon piled up with our supplies and traveling cases.

My uncle told Gretchen that she was in charge of the estate until our return. She kissed her guardian. I could see the tear in her eye when she touched my cheek. I asked her to be my wife.

"Gretchen!" I sighed.

"Go, Alex, go! When you come back I will be your wife," Gretchen said.

I hugged her and took my place in the carriage. Martha and Gretchen, standing at the door, waved their last farewell. Then the horses darted off.

CHAPTER 3
Preparations for Vertical Descent

We soon reached the main railway station. We traveled by train, then steamer, then by small boat until we reached Copenhagen. Finally we arrived at the Phoenix Hotel in Breda Gate. Then we went to the Museum of Northern Antiquities.

My uncle had a letter of introduction to the curator of this establishment. He was the friend of the Danish consul at Hamburg, Professor Thomsen.

We were welcomed cordially. Needless to say we kept the real reason for our trip a secret. Professor Thomsen placed himself at our disposal, and we visited the docks in order to find the next vessel to sail.

I still hoped there would be no way of getting to Iceland. But there was no such luck. A small Danish boat, the *Valkyria,* was to set sail for Reykjavik on the 2nd of June. After the arrangements were made for our passage, we took a tour of the city. But my uncle was only interested in a certain church spire. He insisted we go to the top, more for my benefit than his. He wanted us to be prepared for the awesome heights and depths that we'd encounter on our journey.

At the top, the air made me dizzy. I felt the spire rocking with every gust of wind. My knees began to fail. Soon I was crawling, then creeping on my stomach. I closed my eyes. I seemed to be lost in space. At last, I reached the apex, with my uncle dragging me up by the collar.

"Look down!" he cried. I opened my eyes. My first lesson in dizziness lasted an hour. "Tomorrow we will do it again," said my uncle.

And we did for five days in a row!

The day prior to our departure, Professor Thomsen brought us letters of introduction to Mr. Finsen, mayor of Reykjavik, and Mr. Fridrikssen, a professor. My uncle expressed his gratitude with a hearty handshake.

On June 2nd, at six in the evening, all of our baggage was safely on board the *Valkyria*. The captain took us into a very narrow cabin. We began to sail and in a few days encountered the great Atlantic swell.

When we dropped anchor before Reykjavik, in Faxa Bay, my uncle was enthusiastic. He dragged me forward and pointed north of the bay to a distant mountain with a double peak, which was covered with snow. He cried, "Snaefell!"

My uncle was courteously received by the mayor, Mr. Finsen. Mr. Fridrikssen, professor of natural sciences at the school of Reykjavik, was a delightful man, as well.

Mr. Fridrekssen, the modest philosopher with whom we lodged, spoke only Danish and Latin. In fact, he was the only person in Iceland with whom I could converse at all. This good-natured gentleman let us use two of the three rooms in his house.

"Well, Alex," my uncle said, "now that we are here, I am going to the library. Perhaps there is some manuscript of Saknussemm's there."

Professor Liedenbrock was unusually quiet at dinner. He spoke to me with his eyes as a reminder to keep silent about our plans.

Mr. Fridrikssen wanted to know if my uncle enjoyed his visit to the library and whether he had found what he was looking for. My uncle complained that the shelves were nearly empty. There was not a single text of the works of Arne Saknussemm.

"Arne Saknussemm was persecuted for heresy. His books were burned in

1573," Mr. Fridrikssen explained.

"Now it is all clear," said my uncle, "I see why he had to use a confusing puzzle to hide the secret—"

"What secret?" asked Mr. Fridrikssen. "Have you some private document in your possession?"

"No, I was only imagining," my uncle replied.

"Oh, very well," answered Mr. Fridrikssen, who was kind enough to change the subject. "I hope you will not leave our island until you have seen some of its mineralogical wealth."

"Certainly," replied my uncle. "But surely all has been explored."

"I assure you, Professor, there is plenty left to discover. That mountain in the horizon is Snaefell and is worthy of your time."

"Ah!" said my uncle, as coolly as he could. "Is that Snaefell?"

"Yes. It's one of the most curious volcanoes. Its crater has scarcely ever been visited."

"Well," replied my uncle enthusiastically, "that is where I will begin my studies, there on that Seffel—Fessel—what do you call it?"

"Snaefell," replied Mr. Fridrikssen. "I am very sorry that I can't go with you," he added.

"Oh, no, no!" replied my uncle. "I thank you with all my heart, for the company of such a talented man would have been welcomed. But the duties of

your post at the university must come first."

I was glad Mr. Fridrikssen didn't see through my uncle's transparent remarks.

"Snaefell is a very good choice, Professor. But you will need a guide to take you there. I have one to offer you. He is an inhabitant of that peninsula and is a hunter. He's very clever. He speaks Danish perfectly. You can see him tomorrow."

"Tomorrow, then," added my uncle with a sigh. He was happy to have learned the history of Saknussemm, the reason for the mysterious document, and that our host would not accompany us on the expedition.

CHAPTER 4
A Guide

In the morning, I woke to hear my uncle talking. I dressed and joined him as fast as I could. He was speaking in Danish with a tall man who looked very strong. The man's eyes were sea-blue. He had long hair that fell to his broad shoulders. He was very calm and not animated, unlike my uncle, who couldn't stop moving around. His name was Hans Bjelke.

It wasn't long before they agreed on a payment. Hans would take us to the village of Stapi, on the south shore of the Snaefell peninsula, at the very foot of the volcano. It was a long journey.

We had four horses. Hans knew the

coast perfectly and promised to take us the shortest way.

Once we reached Stapi, Hans was to stay in my uncle's service for the entire expedition.

"Little does he know what marvels await him," my uncle said, sighing.

"So he is to go with us as far as—"

"As far as the center of the earth," my uncle said.

We had two days to pack. This was my

job, unfortunately. All of our supplies, from tools, to arms, to provisions, were to go in four packages. Included in our gear were: a thermometer, a barometer, a chronometer, two compasses, a night glass, two of Ruhmkorff's apparatus, which, by means of an electric current, supplied a safe and handy portable light.

Our tools were two pickaxes, two spades, a silk rope ladder, three iron tipped sticks, a hatchet, a hammer, a dozen wedges and iron spikes, and a long knotted rope. This was a large load, for the ladder was three hundred feet long.

We also took enough food for six months. We didn't take water. We took only empty flasks, since my uncle depended on underground springs to fill them.

There was a fully equipped pocket medicine chest with vials containing a variety of medications.

My uncle took a leathern belt, in which he carried a sufficient quantity of gold, silver, and paper money. We also had six pairs of boots and shoes.

"With these provisions, we can go on forever!" my uncle cried.

On June 15, our preparations were all complete. Mr. Fridrikssen gave my uncle a map of Iceland far more detailed than the one he had. It was a precious document for a mineralogist.

We spent our last evening with our host. It was a restless night for me. At five in the morning I woke to the sound of four neighing horses under my window. I dressed hastily and went down to the street, where Hans finished our packing.

As the final arrangements were completed, Mr. Fridrikssen shook hands with us and bid us a good journey.

CHAPTER 5
A Barren Land

We rode on horseback, and I was becoming excited by the adventure. Saknussemm apparently had traveled at least as far as going down into an extinct crater. We would do it, too.

Hans was in the lead. The next place to stop for the night would be Gardar. I showed my uncle where it was on the map. Three hours later, we reached Gardar.

It should have been night, but in Iceland during the months of June and July, the sun does not set. I was more hungry than cold, and happy to take shelter in a peasant's house where the hospitality was equal to a king's. We stayed the night and departed at five the next morning.

After a few days we began to walk upon hardened lava. Here and there a few jets of steam from hot springs came from now-extinct volcanoes. Soon, at the foot of the mountains, the boggy land reappeared, intersected by little lakes. Our route now lay westward. The twin peaks of Snaefell rose into the cloudy sky five miles away. Although I was getting tired, my uncle and Hans were as fresh as when we started.

On June 20, at six o'clock in the evening, we reached Budir, a village on the seashore. It was Hans's own family who showed us hospitality in Budir. We were well received and I would have liked to stay there, but my uncle wouldn't hear of it. We started off again early the next morning.

As we rounded the immense base of the volcano, my uncle hardly took his eyes off of it. He declared, "There stands

the giant that I shall conquer."

Hans hired the services of three Icelanders to care for the horses and to transport our gear. But as soon as we had arrived at the crater, these natives were to turn back and leave us to our own devices.

My uncle made sure that Hans understood that his intention was to explore the interior of the volcano to its farthest limits. Hans nodded. He would go wherever my uncle directed.

My fears were beginning to rise again since we were now about to climb Snaefell and to explore the crater. Had Saknussemm told a tall tale? Could we lose our way in the deep passages of this volcano? Was Snaefell truly extinct? For the first time on our journey, I expressed my fears to my uncle.

"I was thinking of all that, too," he replied calmly. "For five or six hundred years, Snaefell has been dormant. I can assure you that there will be no eruption."

"But—" I began to say.

"No more on the subject," dictated my uncle. "When science has uttered her voice, let babblers be quiet."

My uncle had an explanation I could not argue with. Perhaps when we had reached the bottom of the crater it would be impossible to find a passage to go deeper!

All night long I had nightmares of being spewed from a volcano.

The next day, Hans and his hired companions were ready and carried our provisions. Hans, being a cautious man, had added a bottle full of water that would last for eight days. We were on our way.

CHAPTER 6
Snaefell at Last

From our starting point we could see Snaefell's two distinct snow-capped cones that stood five thousand feet high.

We walked silently in single file, led by Hans, who ascended the slope on steep, narrow paths. As we traveled, I drew conclusions about how the island came to be. My thoughts suggested that Iceland was produced from the action of internal volcanic fire. To suppose that the internal fire did not still exist was absurd. Nothing could be more absurd than to think that it was possible to reach the earth's center! I felt little comfort as we advanced toward Snaefell.

The way was growing more arduous, the ascent steeper. The loose fragments of rock trembled beneath us. The utmost care was needed to avoid dangerous falls.

Hans went on quietly. Sometimes he would pick up a few bits of stone and build them up into a recognizable form, making landmarks to guide us on our way back.

Three hours later we were still only at the base of the mountain. There we stopped to rest and have a small breakfast.

We then began to scale the steep sides of Snaefell. At some places the elevations were impossible to climb, and we had to help one another with our sticks.

My uncle was surefooted and kept as close to me as possible. He never stumbled. The Icelanders, though burdened with our loads, climbed with agility.

From a distance, the summit looked too difficult to climb. But we were lucky to discover a stairway of misplaced stones that eased our ascent.

By seven, we had ascended the two thousand steps of this grand staircase. We'd reached a bulge in the mountain, a kind of bed on which rested the cone of the crater. Then we encountered a storm and had to take cover from the severe winds and flying rocks. If it weren't for Hans helping us to safety, our mangled bodies would have been carried away to the bottom of the mountain.

Hans did not think it safe to spend the night on the side of the cone. So, we continued our climb. The fifteen hundred remaining feet took us five hours to clear. I could stand it no longer. I was freezing and hungry. I could barely breathe the rarified air.

At last, at eleven in the sunlit night, we reached the summit of Snaefell. The pale rays of the midnight sun shining on the land below were an awesome sight.

CHAPTER 7
Boldly Down the Crater

The next morning, we awoke half-frozen, but warmed by a splendid sun. I rose from my granite bed and went out to enjoy the magnificent spectacle. Then Hans and my uncle joined me on the summit. Hans told us that we were standing on the peak named Scartaris.

My uncle shot a triumphant glance at me. "Now for the crater!" he cried.

In order to make our descent easier, Hans wound his way down the cone by a spiral path. There were glaciers in certain parts of the cone.

At midday we arrived at the bottom of the crater. I raised my head and saw, straight above me, the upper opening of the cone. It framed a bit of sky and was almost perfectly round. Just upon the edge appeared the snowy peak of Saris, standing out sharp and clear against endless space.

At the bottom of the crater were three chimneys, through which lava had long ago erupted. Each of these chimneys had a diameter of a hundred feet. They gaped before us, right in our path. I didn't have the courage to look down any of them. But my uncle had quickly surveyed all three.

"Alex!" my uncle suddenly cried. "Come here and have a look!"

And, sharing his astonishment, I read a name on the western face of the block. The runic characters were half-eroded away.

"Arne Saknussemm!" my uncle read. "Do you believe it now?"

I was silent and returned to my lava seat. Here was crushing evidence. I was

astounded and sat as if in a trance. The Icelanders had been dismissed, and they were now descending the outer slopes of Snaefell to return home.

Hans slept peacefully at the foot of a rock, in a lava bed, where he had found a suitable couch for himself. But my uncle was pacing around the bottom of the crater like a wild beast in a cage. I had neither the desire nor the strength to rise. Following Hans's example, I went off into an unhappy slumber. Thus the first night in the crater passed away.

The next morning a gray, cloudy sky seemed to droop over the summit of the cone. Without the sun to cast a shadow, we wouldn't know which of the craters to descend. My uncle was angry and impatient. The day wore on, and no shadow apeared. Hans did not move from the spot he had selected. My uncle spoke not a word to me.

For the next few days we waited, due to the bad weather. But on the last day of June came a change of weather. The sun poured a flood of light down the crater and showed us that the middle chimney was the one to enter.

"There it is!" shouted my uncle. "Now for the center of the globe!"

"Forut!" Hans said.

"Forward!" repeated my uncle.

CHAPTER 8
Vertical Descent

Now our real journey began. I antici-
pated difficulties at every step. I
stood at the edge but didn't look down.
The hour had come for me to literally
plunge into this adventure. I could refuse
to move forward, but I was ashamed to
do so in front of Hans, who accepted the
adventure with such calmness. For a
moment I thought of Gretchen, then I
approached the central chimney.

My hair stood on end as I stared down
the deep shaft. The walls of the cone
were perpendicular. There were rocks
jutting from each side, which would help
the descent, but there was still no rail. A
rope fastened to the edge of the opening

would help us down. But how were we to unfasten it when we arrived at the other end? There wasn't a rope in the world long enough for this task.

My uncle came up with a solution by uncoiling a cord that was four hundred feet long. He dropped half of it down, then he passed it around a lava block. Then he threw the other half down the chimney. Each of us could then descend by holding both halves of the rope,

which would not be able to unroll itself from its hold. When we were two hundred feet down, it would be easy to get hold of the whole of the rope by letting one end go and pulling down by the other. We would repeat these steps until we reached the bottom. We divided our supplies and began the descent.

Down we went. The bottom of the hole was not visible. After a long time, we came to a small ledge where we stopped.

Then we repeated our movements. My uncle said to me, "The farther I go, the more confident I feel. The order of these volcanic formations suggests that the theory of central heat is nonsense. We shall see further proof soon."

After another three hours, I still saw no bottom to the chimney. We had descended 2,800 feet. I had kept track of how many times we used the rope to complete my calculations.

Suddenly, Hans cried, "Halt!"

I stopped short just as I was going to place my feet upon my uncle's head.

"We are there," my uncle cried.

"Where?" I asked.

"At the bottom of the chimney," he answered.

"Is there no way farther?" I asked.

"Yes, there is a passage that inclines to the right. We will explore it tomorrow. Let's have supper and go to sleep," my uncle instructed.

CHAPTER 9

The Wonders of Terrestrial Depths

In the morning, a ray of daylight shone on the surfaces of lava on the walls like a shower of sparks. We could see our surroundings.

"The quietness down here is alarming," I said.

"We haven't even begun and already you are frightened," my uncle replied.

"What do you mean?" I asked.

"We are only at sea level," my uncle explained. "I consulted the barometer."

In fact, the mercury, which had risen in the instrument as fast as we descended, had stopped at twenty-nine inches.

"You see," my uncle said, "we have now

only the pressure of our atmosphere. This instrument will become useless as soon as the weight of the atmosphere exceeds the pressure at sea level."

"But won't all of the ever-increasing pressure become very painful?" I asked.

"No, we shall descend at a slow rate, and our lungs will become used to a denser atmosphere," my uncle replied.

After breakfast, my uncle took a small notebook from his pocket. He consulted his instruments and recorded the pressure, temperature and our location.

"Now we are really heading into the interior of the earth! From this point our journey really starts!" my uncle cried as he headed into a tunnel.

My uncle took the Ruhmkorff's apparatus and formed an electric current with the coil in the lantern. A bright light lit the dark passage. Hans carried the other lantern. These artificial lights would be safe even in the center of the most inflammable gases.

"Let's go!" my uncle said. I was last as we entered the dark gallery.

The dried lava shone brilliantly in the light while we lowered our baggage before us from the end of a long rope. We went down the gentle slope carefully.

The lava, which was porous in many places, had formed a surface covered with small, rounded blisters. There were crystals of opaque quartz hanging like chandeliers from the roof. Stalactites were overhead.

"This is magnificent!" I cried.

"You will see greater splendors than these, I'm sure," my uncle said.

We dropped down the steep inclines. According to the compass, which I consulted frequently, our direction was southeast. The lava stream deviated neither to the right nor to the left.

Two hours after our departure there was only a small increase in temperature. I began to believe that our descent was more horizontal than vertical. My uncle measured the exact depth we had reached, but he kept the results to himself.

At about eight in the evening we stopped. We were in a sort of cavern, where there was plenty of air. Puffs of it reached us, but what caused them we didn't know. Hunger and fatigue made me incapable of reasoning. I was exhausted after seven hours of descent. But one thing troubled me—our supply

of water was half-consumed.

"Don't be alarmed that we have not found springs," my uncle said. "We shall find more than we want."

"When?" I asked.

"When we leave these thick walls of lava. Water can't break through them," he explained.

"But perhaps this path runs deep. We haven't progressed down it very far," I said. "It would be hotter if we had gone deeper."

"According to your system," my uncle said. "But what does the thermometer say?"

"It has changed only slightly since our departure," I answered.

"Well, what is your conclusion?" he asked.

"Based on my observations and the change in temperature indicated by the thermometer, we have gone a depth of 1,125 feet," I said.

"By my observations we are at ten thousand feet below the level of the sea," my uncle said.

His calculations were correct. We had already attained a depth of six thousand feet beyond that ever reached by man.

The temperature, which ought to have been 178°F, was scarcely 59°F. Perhaps there were no internal fires!

We continued our descent the next day at 6 a.m.

We were still following the gallery of lava, a real natural staircase, until my uncle exclaimed, "We are at the very end of the chimney."

We were standing at the intersection of two roads, both dark and narrow. Which were we to take? My uncle refused to admit that he was confused. He pointed to the eastern tunnel, and we were soon in it.

Sometimes the passageway narrowed and we had to creep along through it. The heat was bearable, and I hoped that this so-called extinct volcano wouldn't become active again.

By six in the evening, after a fairly easy walk, we had gone two leagues south, but barely a quarter of a mile down. We ate our supper quietly and went to bed.

The next morning we awoke fresh and in good spirits. We again followed the path of the lava. But it seemed as if we were going up, not down. My uncle did not want to admit it and was very angry.

By midday the appearance of the

rocks changed. "We are moving away from the primary granite," I said. "We are at the period when the first plants and animals appeared."

We hadn't gone far before I saw evidence. My feet, which had become accustomed to the lava floor, suddenly rested on dust composed of the debris of plants and shells. I picked up a shell and said, "Look at this!"

"Very well," my uncle said quietly, "it is the shell of a crustacean, of an extinct

species. Nothing more."

"But don't you conclude—?"

"Yes, I admit that I may have been mistaken. But I cannot be sure of that until I have reached the very end of this gallery."

"That is wise except for one danger," I said. "We are running out of water."

"Then we must begin to ration our supply," he said.

We barely had enough water for three days, and there was hardly a chance

that we'd find a natural spring. In silence, we explored the endless arcades of the gallery the whole next day. Hans's demeanor was rubbing off on us.

The greater part of the walls bore impressions of primitive organisms. It was evident that we were ascending that scale of animal life in which man fills the highest place. But my uncle didn't seem to notice it.

Suddenly, at six o'clock, we reached a wall that blocked our path. "Very well, it's all right!" my uncle cried. "We are not on Saknussemm's road. All we have to do is to go back. Let's rest for the night. In three days we shall get back to the fork in the road."

"Yes," I said, "if we have any strength left. Tomorrow we won't have any water."

We started early the next day and moved swiftly. We soon ran out of water, and the air and temperature overcame us.

At last, six days later, we arrived, half-

dead, at the junction of the two roads.
There I dropped like a lifeless lump.

"Drink!" my uncle said. He gave me
the last sip of water from his flask.

"Thank you," I said. Although my
thirst was only partially quenched, some
strength had returned. "We must go
back," I said. "It is the only thing to do."

"Return?" said my uncle. "Just when
we have the best chance of success?
Never!"

"Then we will surely die!" I cried.

"You go back. Hans will go with you. Leave me here!" my uncle said.

"No, I cannot do that," I said.

My uncle was very excited. His voice had become hard and threatening. Hans was resigned to following him to the end.

"I examined the gallery while you were unconscious," my uncle said. "It goes downward. In a few hours it will bring us to the granite rocks where there are many springs. I am sure of it. If, in a single day, I have not found water, we will return to the surface of the earth."

CHAPTER 10
Total Failure of Water

This time the descent was in a new gallery. Hans walked first. We had not gone a hundred yards when my uncle, moving his lantern along the walls, cried, "Here are primitive rocks. Now we are going the right way. Forward!"

The light from our lanterns, reflected from the small facets of quartz, shot sparkling rays at every angle. I seemed to be moving through a diamond. We saw traces of platinum and gold. At about six o'clock these colorful splendors almost stopped. We were within prison walls of granite.

By eight in the evening there were still no signs of water. I was horribly thirsty.

My uncle strode on. He refused to stop. He was listening anxiously for the murmur of distant springs. The deadline was almost upon us.

At last I fell. My uncle gazed upon me with his arms crossed. "It's all over!" he raged as I closed my eyes.

When I reopened my eyes, I saw my two companions sleeping in their rolls. A deep silence reigned around us. No sound could reach us through the walls, the thinnest of which were five miles thick. Then, in the midst of my illusions, I thought I saw Hans moving out of sight with the lamp in his hand. Was he abandoning us?

But at last I heard footsteps in the dark abyss. Hans was returning.

"Watten!" said Hans, pointing downward. He had found evidence of water!

We hurried down the passageway. In an hour we had gone a mile and a quarter, and descended two thousand feet. Then I heard the sound of something running within the thick granite wall like distant thunder.

"Hans is correct," my uncle said. "That is the sound of a rushing torrent. An underground river is flowing around us!"

Hans examined a wall of granite to find the exact place where the torrent could be heard the loudest. He found it and selected a pickax. But would using it break the wall and cause a flood or cause the earth to collapse on top of us? Our thirst was so intense that we had to chance it.

The pickax had soon penetrated two feet into the granite wall. Hans had worked for more than an hour. Suddenly, we heard a hiss and a jet of water spurted out against the opposite wall. Hans was almost knocked off of his feet. He uttered a painful cry.

"The water is boiling!" I cried.

"Well, let it cool," replied my uncle.

The tunnel was filling with steam while a stream was forming. Soon we had the satisfaction of swallowing our first drink. We drank without stopping. It was water high in iron and as good as any found in a spa.

"It is delicious!" I cried.

"What a wonderful source of strength Hans has found," my uncle said. "We shall name the water after him."

"Agreed," I cried.

And Hansbach it was from that moment. We filled our flasks and then tried to block the hole, but the pressure was too great. We decided to allow the water to flow so that it would continue throughout the passage and we'd have a regular supply of it.

"With this stream for our guide, there is no reason why we should not succeed," I said.

"Ah, my boy! You agree with me now," my uncle cried, laughing.

"I agree with you most heartily," I said.

"Well, let us rest awhile. Then we will start again," my uncle advised.

The next day at 8 a.m., we started afresh. The granite tunnel, winding from side to side, led us past unexpected turns, and seemed almost to form a maze. My uncle never ceased to consult his compass to keep account of the ground gone over. He was annoyed that the road was mainly horizontal and did not take us down deeper into the earth. On the whole, that day and the next we

made considerable way horizontally, but very little vertically.

The next evening, we were thirty leagues southeast of Reykjavik, and at a depth of two and a half leagues.

At our feet was a frightful abyss. My uncle was not to be daunted. He was excited by the steepness of the descent. "This will take us a long way," he cried. "And without much difficulty, as the projections in the rock form quite a staircase."

Hans fastened ropes so as to guard us against accident. The descent began.

This well, or abyss, was a narrow fault in the mass of the granite. We kept going down a kind of winding staircase, which seemed almost to have been made by man.

We stopped every fifteen minutes. We then sat down upon a fragment of rock and talked as we ate and drank from the stream. The Hansbach fell in a cascade, and lost some of its volume. But there was enough to quench our thirst.

Five days later, we were seven leagues underground and had traveled fifty leagues away from Snaefell. Although we were tired, our health was perfect. My uncle checked his instruments every hour. Iceland was behind us, and we were now under the ocean. Four days later we arrived at a vast grotto.

CHAPTER 11

Out of the Deep

We were getting used to living underground and no longer thought
about life on the surface. The grotto was
an immense apartment with a cool water
stream running along its floor.

After breakfast, my uncle worked on
his notes. He wanted to map the path of
our expedition so others could do it, too.
We again debated the theory of internal
heat and also talked about the dangers
of the increasing pressure as we
descended. My uncle had me again
check the thermometer only to discover
that the temperature was not increasing
as I'd thought it would.

I still held to the theory of central

heat, although I did not feel its effects. I preferred to admit, in truth, that this chimney of an extinct volcano did not let the heat pass through its walls. I also thought that the air, due to immense pressure, would become a solid once we reached a certain depth. We would reach a point at which we could go no farther.

But I did not argue. My uncle would only have reminded me of Saknussemm's descent. I questioned Saknussemm's success, though. In the sixteenth century there were no instruments to measure how far to the center of the earth he had actually gone.

The rest of the day was passed in calculations and in conversations. I had to admit that things were not going badly. With continued luck we might hope to reach our end and scientific glory! I was beginning to sound like my uncle! Each day we advanced nearly two leagues encountering steeper declines. Some were nearly straight down. We could

never have managed these without Hans.

On one of our descents I was examining the beds of granite. Suddenly I was alone.

I retraced my steps, walking for a quarter of an hour. I shouted. There was no reply. "Be calm!" I said aloud to myself. "There are not two roads. I was too far ahead. I will return!"

For half an hour I climbed up and heard nothing. I stopped. I could not believe that I was lost. The flow of the spring would now have to be my guide. I stooped to bathe my face in the Hansbach. To my surprise and dismay, my feet were on dry granite! The stream was no longer at my feet.

I was in total despair, buried alive. How was I to return? There were no footprints to follow. I was doomed!

I had three days' provisions with me, and my flask was full. But I could not remain alone for long. Should I go up or

down? I decided to go up continually to the point where I had left the stream. With the stream at my feet, I might hope to regain the summit of Snaefell.

For half an hour I walked through the gallery, but didn't recognize anything. Then the gallery came to an abrupt end. I hit an impenetrable wall and fell down on a rock. I shattered my lamp and was lying in the heavy gloom of darkness.

I arose with my arms stretched out

before me, attempting painfully to feel my way. I began to run wildly, hurrying through the maze, still descending. I hit my head on a jagged rock, and my face became covered with blood. After a few hours, I fell like a lifeless lump at the foot of a wall and lost all consciousness.

When I awoke, my face was wet with tears. I don't know how long I had been unconscious. I felt weak from the loss of blood that I suffered. I gathered my

strength and rolled to the foot of the opposite wall where I heard Hans's voice and then my uncle's.

"Uncle!" I shouted.

I waited anxiously. Sound does not travel with great speed, even in the denser air. Seconds, which seemed like hours, passed.

"Alex, where are you?" my uncle finally asked.

"I am lost in the darkness," I said. "We must find out how far apart we are. Say my name and note the exact second on your chronometer. I will repeat it as soon as I hear it. Observe the exact moment that you get my answer."

"Half the time between my call and your answer will indicate how long my voice will take in coming to you," my uncle said.

I put my ear to the wall and, as soon as the name "Alex" came, I immediately replied "Alex," then waited.

"Forty seconds," my uncle said. "So

the sound takes twenty seconds to reach me. Now, at the rate of 1,120 feet a second, this is 22,400 feet, or nearly four and a quarter miles."

I began my descent. The slope was rapid, and I slid down. Suddenly there was no ground under me. I felt myself revolving in air, striking against the craggy projections of a vertical gallery. My head struck against a sharp corner of the rock, and I became unconscious.

When I came to, I was covered with thick coats and blankets. My uncle was watching over me.

"He is alive!" he cried tenderly.

I wanted to know what day it was, but my uncle insisted that I rest. I was very weak and went to sleep. I didn't realize that I had been alone in the heart of the earth for four long days!

The next morning when I woke, I wondered if I was dreaming or crazed by my fall. It seemed I saw natural light and heard the murmuring of waves and the wind. Could we have returned to the earth's surface? Was our expedition over? I was asking myself these questions when my uncle entered.

"Good morning," he cried cheerily. "I hope you are better."

"Yes, I am," I said, sitting up.

My uncle gave me a small meal while he told me how we came to be reunited. "It is a miracle that you weren't killed," my uncle said. "We must be careful never to separate again."

"Isn't the journey over?" I asked. "I must be mad. Isn't that light and wind and the sound of the sea?"

"I can't explain, but you will soon see and understand that geology has not yet learned all it has to learn," he answered.

"Then let us go see," I said quickly.

"No, the open air might be bad for you so soon," my uncle warned.

"But I am fine," I assured him.

"A little patience, my nephew. A relapse might get us into trouble, and we have no time to lose. The voyage may be a long one."

"The voyage!" I cried.

"Rest today, and tomorrow we will set sail," he said.

"Set sail!" I said. My impatience was so strong that my uncle finally gave in. I dressed and went out of the grotto.

CHAPTER 12
An Internal Sea

At first I could hardly see. My eyes had to adjust to the light. When they did, I was shocked. "The sea!" I cried.

"Yes," my uncle replied, "the Liedenbrock Sea. I'm sure no one will mind my claim to name it, since I discovered it."

Before me was a vast sea. Small shells, which had been inhabited by earth's first beings, were strewn about. About one hundred fathoms from the limit of the waves was a huge wall of vast cliffs. It was of enormous height and was wild in appearance.

Within the cavern was a peculiar light like an aurora borealis. It filled the sky.

The sky seemed composed of vast plains of clouds, shifting and filled with vapor that inevitably would cause rain.

We walked along the shore, and my attention was drawn to an unexpected sight. It was a forest of mushrooms that had grown very large, due to living in the moist, warm climate. Some were thirty to forty feet high and were crowned with a cap of equal diameter. There were thousands of them.

Farther on rose groups of tall trees with colorless foliage. They were the shrubs of earth, and here, attaining gigantic size.

"Wonderful, magnificent, splendid!" my uncle cried. "Here is the entire flora of the second period of the earth—the transition period. Look, there are also bones of extinct animals!"

I rushed to see the bones. There was a lower jaw of a mastodon and the femur of the megatherium! How could this be, I wondered? How could these creatures have come to live under the earth's surface? Would we encounter live beasts?

I felt tired, and we went to sit down at the end of a cape, at the foot of which the waves came and beat themselves into spray. After spending an hour looking at these marvelous sights, we returned to the shore of the grotto.

CHAPTER 13
Preparations for a Voyage of Discovery

I felt much better the next morning. I swam for a while in the marvelous sea. We had breakfast, and Hans was able to make coffee. It was the most delicious coffee we had ever had.

"We must not miss the high tide," my uncle said excitedly.

"I can't believe my eyes," I cried. "It is extraordinary that under this terrestrial crust, there is an ocean with ebbing and flowing tides, with winds and storms."

"Well," my uncle replied, "is there any scientific reason against it?"

"No, not if you disregard the theory of central heat," I admitted.

"So then, so far, I am correct," he said.

"I guess so," I admitted.

"It might be inhabited, too," my uncle said.

"We might be able to fish these seas," I suggested.

I began to wonder where, beneath the earth's surface, we were exactly. "Uncle, what do your instruments show our location to be?" I asked.

"Horizontally, three hundred and fifty leagues from Iceland," he answered. "I

can't be more than one mile off. I have noticed that the needle of my compass, instead of dipping toward the pole as in the northern hemisphere, rises from it."

"Then the magnetic pole is somewhere between the surface of the globe and the point where we are," I said. "What depth have we now reached?"

"We are thirty-five leagues below the surface."

"So," I said, examining the map,

"Scotland is over our heads. But now what are your plans? Are you thinking of returning to the surface?"

"We will not return! We will continue our journey, everything having gone on well so far," he said.

"How do you propose to get below the sea?" I asked.

"If all oceans are actually lakes encompassed by land, this internal sea will be surrounded by a granite coast. We'll walk its shores and find fresh passages opening along it. We should set sail tomorrow," he said.

"Aboard what kind of boat?" I wondered aloud.

"It will be a well-made raft. Hans has been working on it already," my uncle said.

We found Hans at work making a raft of fossil wood. By the next evening, the raft was complete.

CHAPTER 14
Wonders of the Deep

We awoke very early the next day. We were ready to travel by sea, which would be faster and less tiring than our previous method. Two poles spliced together formed a mast, and a blanket was a sail. We loaded all of our provisions, and Hans took the tiller. We set sail. At the moment of leaving the harbor, we decided to call it Port Gretchen.

Due to the dense atmosphere, we moved swiftly. We expected to see the opposite shore within one day. It wasn't long before we could no longer see the shore behind us, nor the one before us.

Immense shoals of seaweed came into view. These were three or four thousand

feet long, waving like serpents. I watched
them for hours, and wondered what natural force could have produced such
plants.

We traveled fast and far due to the
winds, but still we couldn't see the
opposite shore before us. We had no
way of knowing if Saknusseumm had
also traveled this sea.

On another day, my uncle dropped
our anchor to see how far it was to the

bottom of this ocean. But even after lowering the anchor more than two hundred fathoms, we didn't reach the bottom. When he pulled it up, however, it did bear the imprint of teeth, as if a huge undersea creature had bitten it! We were on our guard from that moment on.

There was no darkness here. It was as if we were sailing under the Arctic sun. One day, a terrible shock awoke me. The raft was heaved up on a watery mountain and pitched down again, at a distance of twenty fathoms.

"What is the matter?" my uncle shouted. "Have we struck land?"

Hans pointed with his finger at a dark mass six hundred yards away, rising and falling alternately with heavy plunges.

I looked and cried, "It is an enormous porpoise."

"Yes," my uncle replied with shock. "There is also a giant sea lizard! And farther on is a monstrous crocodile.

Look at its large jaws and its rows of teeth! It is diving down!"

"There's a whale!" I cried. "I can see his great fins. See how he is throwing out air and water through his blowers."

We stood amazed at the presence of such a herd of marine monsters. They were of supernatural dimensions. The smallest of them would have crunched our raft, crew and all, with one snap of its huge jaws.

Hans wanted to get away from this dangerous area. He saw other creatures that could threaten us on the other side of our raft. There was a forty-foot-long tortoise and a thirty-foot serpent. There seemed to be no limit to the marvels .

These creatures encircled our raft. Then they began to fight amongst themselves. My uncle, through his telescopic glass, saw that the beast with the porpoise's snout and crocodile's teeth was really an plesiosaur, a prehistoric fish lizard. It was the most terrible of the ancient monsters of the deep.

"And the other?" I asked with disbelief.

"The other is an ichthyosaur, a lizard-like serpent," he answered. "He is the dreadful enemy of the other."

Those huge creatures attacked each other, rocking our raft in the waves they created. Suddenly they disappeared below the water, leaving a whirlpool eddying in the water. Several minutes passed while the fight continued underwater.

All at once the enormous head of the plesiosaur darted up. The monster was wounded to death. As for the ichthyosaur, we never saw it again.

The wind blew violently as we left the scene of the primitive struggle. Hans was still at the helm. My uncle, no longer distracted by the combat, began again to look impatiently around him. The voyage to the other side of the sea was longer than expected.

The wind was unsteady and fitful.

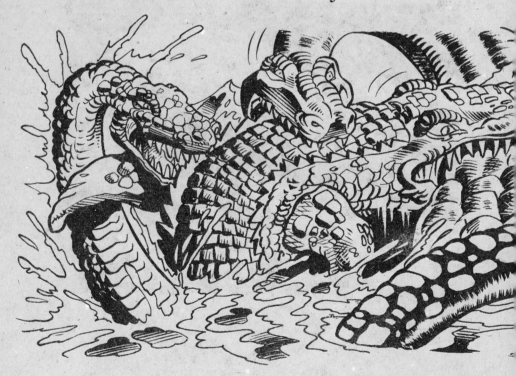

The temperature was high. At about noon we heard a distant continuous roar.

"In the distance there is a rock, against which the sea is breaking," my uncle said.

I heard roaring that seemed to come from a very distant waterfall. I hoped we wouldn't be thrown over it! Hans climbed the mast to take a look.

"He sees something," my uncle said. "I see it, too. It is a vast, inverted cone

rising from the surface."

"If it is another sea beast, let's get out of its path," I said.

"Let us go straight on!" my uncle yelled.

I appealed to Hans, but he maintained his course inflexibly.

At eight in the evening we were only two leagues from it. Its enormous body was spread upon the sea like an island. We were getting near a monster that could eat a hundred whales a day!

Terror seized me, but my uncle would not give in.

"Geyser," Hans said.

"It is a geyser, like those in Iceland," my uncle said.

At first I couldn't believe that I had mistaken an island for a monster. The geyser rose majestically. Deep and heavy explosions were heard from time to time. The enormous jet spouted water until it reached the clouds.

"Let's dock," my uncle said. "But we must avoid this waterspout. It would sink our raft in a moment."

My uncle and I climbed onto the island while Hans stayed at the raft. We reached the central basin, out of which the geyser came. I plunged a thermometer into the boiling water. It marked an intense heat far above the boiling point. This water came from a furnace. Was this proof of the earth's central heat? My uncle wouldn't admit it.

Still, it seemed to me that someday we would reach a region where the earth's central heat attained its highest limits. It would go beyond a point that can be registered by our thermometers.

"We shall see," my uncle said. He named this island after me.

We left the island after Hans refitted the raft's rudder. By my observations we had crossed two hundred and seventy leagues of sea since leaving Port Gretchen. We were six hundred and twenty leagues away from Iceland.

CHAPTER 15

An Electric Storm

A few days later, the magnificent geyser had disappeared and the wind had carried us away from Alex Island. The atmosphere was charged with vapors. I felt a peculiar sensation. My hair bristled, and it seemed as if my companions would receive a severe shock if they touched me.

"There's a heavy storm coming on!" I cried, pointing toward the horizon. "Those clouds seem as if they are going to crush the sea."

A deep silence fell on all of us. My uncle's temper was awful.

"Let us reef the sail and cut the mast down!" I cried. "That will be safest."

"No! Never!" my uncle shouted. "Let the wind catch us if it will! What I want is to get the least glimpse of rock or shore, even if our raft should be smashed!"

The mast held firm, but the sail stretched tight like a bubble ready to burst.

"The sail!" I cried, motioning to my uncle and Hans to lower it.

"No!" my uncle replied.

No!" Hans repeated, shaking his head.

Vivid flashes of lightning mingled with the violent crash of continuous thunder. Ceaseless fiery arrows darted in and out amongst the flying clouds. The vaporous mass soon glowed with heat. Hailstones rattled fiercely down, and as they hit iron tools, they, too, emitted gleams and flashes of light. My eyes failed under the dazzling light. I tied myself to the mast, which bowed like a reed before the mighty strength of the storm. The violent storm made it impossible for me to keep track of our adventure from that point onward. My notes became very sketchy.

By the next day, we didn't know where we were. The storm would not let up. Our ears bled from the pressure. We didn't speak, since we couldn't hear one another. The lightning flashes kept striking the granite vault over our heads. What if it caved in on us? The heat increased.

By the next day, we had traveled two hundred leagues from Alex Island. At

noon, the violence of the storm doubled. We secured all of our cargo. Each of us was tied to some part of the raft, since the waves rose above our heads.

We traveled like this for three days. At last I wrote down the words "Let us lower the sail." My uncle finally consented.

Then a ball of fire bounded over the waves and landed on board our raft. The mast and sail flew up in flames at once.

We lay there, our blood running cold with unspeakable terror. The fireball

was half-white and half-blue. It was the size of a ten-inch shell and moved slowly about the raft. It revolved on its own axis with astonishing speed.

Then the dazzling disk of mysterious light nimbly leaped aside and approached Hans. Then it threatened my uncle, who fell upon his knees with his head down to avoid it. And then my turn came. I was pale and trembling under the blinding splendor and the melting heat. It dropped at my feet, spinning silently around upon the deck. I tried to move my foot away but couldn't.

A suffocating smell of nitrogen filled the air and entered our throats and lungs. We suffered stifling pains. I was unable to move my foot. It seemed to be stuck to the planks. That electric globe that fell on our raft had magnetized everything on board! The nails of my boots clung to the iron plate on the raft. All of the iron instruments on board clinked and clashed against one another.

Then the globe exploded into fire, and the light disappeared.

The storm continued to roar and rage. We were at the sea's mercy and were moving at an incalculable speed. We had been carried under England, and under France, and perhaps under the whole of Europe!

Then the raft was suddenly dashed upon the jagged rocks of the shore. The only thing that saved us was Hans's strong arm. Hans went back into the

furious waves to try to save whatever he could. Though he was able to rescue our provisions, we could hardly eat because we were so tired from three sleepless nights.

The next day, the weather had improved. The sky and the sea were calm. No trace of the storm existed. I awoke to hear my uncle chattering happily.

If only our raft had gone a bit farther east, we would now be under Hamburg, under the very street where my dear love, Gretchen, safely resided. But we were forty leagues perpendicular of solid granite wall, and a thousand leagues under!

"How did you sleep?" my uncle asked.

"Well enough," I said. "You seem in very good spirits this morning, Uncle."

"Why, I'm delighted, my boy. We are there," he said.

"To our journey's end?" I asked.

"No, to the end of that sea. Now we shall go by land and really begin to go down!" he replied.

I could not believe that my uncle still wanted to continue. "How will we ever return?" I asked.

"In the simplest way possible. When we have reached the center of the globe, either we shall find some new way to get back, or we shall come back the way we came," my uncle explained.

"Do we have enough food to last?" I asked.

"Yes. I'm sure Hans saved everything

he could. Let's see," he replied.

Hans was surrounded by what he had saved. It was all in good order. My uncle thanked him. Hans seemed to have a superhuman devotion to my uncle. He must have worked the entire time we slept, risking his own life.

"Here are the thermometers and the chronometer," my uncle said. "Hans is a splendid fellow."

There was no denying it. We had all of our instruments, tools, and appliances.

Hans was even able to save some of our food. We had biscuits, salted meat, and salted fish—nearly four months' supply.

"Now," my uncle said, "we will replenish our water supply with the rain that the storm has left. As for the raft, I recommend Hans do his best to repair it, although I don't expect it will be of any further use to us. And now let us go to breakfast."

"Where are we now, Uncle?" I asked as we ate.

"We have come a good long way. But whether we are under Turkey or the Atlantic depends very much upon in what direction we have been moving. Perhaps we have deviated," my uncle said.

My uncle moved toward the rock and looked at the compass. Then he turned to me thunderstruck with some unexpected discovery.

"What is the matter?" I asked, taking a look at the compass myself.

It seemed that during the storm there had been a sudden change of wind unperceived by us. It had brought our raft back to the shore, which we thought we had left so far behind us!

My uncle was mystified, then enraged. We had gone backward instead of forward! We'd have to cross the sea again.

The Liedenbrock Museum
of Geology

"I will not yield," he shouted. "I will not stir a single foot backward. It will be seen whether man or nature is to have the upper hand!"

"It would be mad to attempt a second crossing," I said. "Our raft is broken, the sail torn, we can't steer." My uncle was deaf to my speech.

"We shall sail tomorrow," he said. "I must neglect nothing. Since my fate has driven me to this part of the coast, I will not leave it until I have examined it."

To understand what followed, it must be known that we were not really where my uncle thought we were. We left Hans to his work while we walked toward the wall of rock. There we found shells of all shapes and sizes and the shells that had covered gigantic glyptodons and armadillos of the Pleistocene period. The soil was scattered with stony fragments and boulders.

We walked upon sedimentary soil, the deposits of the waters of former ages. My uncle carefully examined every fissure in the rocks. Wherever he saw a hole he always wanted to know its depth.

We walked along the shores of the Liedenbrock Sea for a mile. We then observed a sudden change in the appearance of the soil. Within three square miles we saw the materials for a complete history of the animal life of all the ages. I stood amazed. My uncle did, too. Then he placed his hand upon a bare skull and cried with a voice that trembled with excitement, "A human head!"

"A human skull?" I cried. I was as

astonished as he was to find evidence of a humanlike fossil that came from one of the earliest periods of geological history. This discovery would amaze scholars worldwide!

My uncle was in a state of frenzied excitement when, twenty yards ahead, he found himself face-to-face with the dried corpse of a primitive man! It was a perfectly recognizable human body. This fossil body was not the only one in this immense catacomb. We came upon more bodies at every step.

It was quite a sight, this cemetery of human and animal bones. We wondered how all of these bones came to be in this same spot. Had there been a fissure into which they slid into the crust of the earth to land on the shores of the Liedenbrock Sea? Did they live in this subterranean world?

Until this point of our journey, we had seen only live marine monsters and fishes. Might not some living man, some native of the abyss, be here, too?

CHAPTER 17
Electric Illumination

For another half hour we walked upon a pavement of bones. We were filled with curiosity. I was prepared for any surprise.

We advanced in silence, bathed in light from luminous electric fluid that coated all around us. By some unexplainable phenomenon, it lit up all sides of every object equally. We were men without shadows.

After walking a mile, we reached the outskirts of a vast forest. There was a soft carpet of moss and a few sparkling streams. But there was no color or scent to any of the plants. I wondered, if nature had provided vegetable nourishment here, wouldn't there be mammals, too? Suddenly I halted and I drew back my uncle.

I saw vast colossal forms moving amongst the trees. It was a herd of mastodons—not fossil remains, but living specimens! I heard the crashing noises they made as they walked. My earlier dreams of live creatures of the prehistoric world were now realized!

"Look!" my uncle then said suddenly.

At a distance of a quarter of a mile

stood a human being watching this herd of mastodons like a shepherd! It was a giant! He was at least twelve feet tall. His head, huge and unshapely, was half-hidden in the thick and tangled growth of his unkempt hair. He wielded an enormous bough like a staff to manage his herd.

We stood petrified and speechless with amazement. What if he saw us? We had to get away from there!

In another quarter of an hour we were beyond the reach of this creature.

It is absurd to believe that humans lived in this underground world with no connection to the inhabitants on its surface! It may have been some animal whose structure resembled that of a human. But that a man, a living man, and therefore whole generations doubtless besides, should be there in the bowels of the earth was impossible.

We left behind the luminous forest, dumb with astonishment. We kept running on for fear the creature might be on our track.

As we moved on, we realized that we had returned to the north of the Liedenbrock Sea.

Our surroundings were foreign, and yet seemed familiar at the same time. I thought I recognized the bed of fossil wood Hans used to make our raft, the *Hansbach*, and the grotto in which I had recovered. Then a few paces ahead we encountered a strange stream, then cliffs that didn't look like those at Port Gretchen. My uncle agreed; he didn't recognize anything, either.

"Evidently," I said, "we have not landed at our original starting point. The storm must have carried us a little higher. If we follow the shore, we'll find Port Gretchen."

"If that is the case, it will be useless to continue our exploration. We'd better return to our raft," my uncle said. "But, Alex, are you sure you're not mistaken?"

"I don't know for sure," I said. "All of these rocks are so much alike. Yet I think I recognize the cape where Hans constructed our raft. We must be very near the port, if indeed this is not it."

"But we should at least find traces of our own activities here," my uncle said.

"I do see something," I cried, darting upon an object lying on the sand. I showed my uncle a rusty dagger, which I had just picked up.

"Did you have this weapon with you?" he asked.

"No, but maybe you did," I suggested.

"Not that I am aware of," my uncle said.

"Well, this is strange!" I sighed.

"No, it is very simple," my uncle said. "The Icelanders often wear arms of this kind. This must have belonged to Hans, and he has lost it."

I shook my head. I knew that Hans had never had an object like this in his possession.

"Maybe it belonged to some living man like the one we saw in the forest,"

I suggested. "But, no, this is not a relic of the stone age. It is not even of the iron age. This blade is steel."

My uncle stopped me abruptly. "This is a sixteenth-century dagger. It was never yours, mine or Hans's. It didn't belong to any of those human beings who may or may not inhabit this inner world." My uncle was getting excited and was allowing his imagination to run away with him.

"We are on the way toward the grand

discovery. This blade has been here for hundreds of years!" he cried.

"But it didn't get here by itself. Someone has been here before us!" I exclaimed.

"A man who has engraved his name somewhere with that dagger to mark the way to the center of the earth! Let us look!" he said.

We walked along a steep cliff and found a passage no wider than a couple of yards. Between two boldly projecting rocks we found the mouth of a dark tunnel. There, upon a granite slab, appeared two etched letters, half eaten away by time. They were the initials of the bold and daring traveler.

"A. S.!" my uncle shouted. "You see? Arne Saknussemm!"

CHAPTER 18
Blasting a Passage to the Center of the Earth

These two letters, engraved on this spot hundreds of years ago, shocked me. It was astounding! I could no longer doubt Arne Saknussemm's existence or the fact that he had made this incredible journey nearly four hundred years before us.

My uncle was ecstatic and decided to call the spot Cape Saknussemm.

I forgot all of our past perils and the future danger of our return. If Saknussemm had done it, so could we. We returned to get Hans and the raft.

"Now we shall go down! It is now only 1,500 leagues to the center of the globe," my uncle said

"Let's get started!" I cried.

Hans had made everything ready for our instant departure. We took our places and set off.

The wind was not favorable, however. Sometimes the water was too shallow to pass easily over. At last, after three hours of sailing, we reached a place to land. I jumped ashore, followed by my uncle and Hans. I was still ready to keep going forward.

My uncle switched on his Ruhmkorff's apparatus. We tied the raft to the shore. The mouth of the tunnel was only twenty yards from us. We headed for it without a moment's delay.

The opening, which was almost round, was about five feet in diameter. The dark passage was cut out in the live rock. It was lined with a coat of the eruptive matter. The interior was level with the ground outside, so that we were able to enter without difficulty.

We were suddenly halted by an enormous blockage. There was no way around it. I was disappointed. My uncle paced from side to side in the narrow passage.

"But how did Saknussemm get around it?" I asked.

"Was he stopped by this barrier of stone?" my uncle wondered.

"No," I replied. I could tell by the rock and its position that it had fallen after Saknussemm traveled here and that this gallery was once open. "If we don't destroy it, we won't reach the center of the earth."

"Let's try our pickaxes, or the spade," my uncle cried.

"That would take us too long. Let's mine the obstacle and blow it up," I said without hesitation.

"Oh, yes, it is only a bit of rock to blast! Hans, to work!" my uncle said.

I was very excited. While Hans worked

to prepare a hole for the gunpowder, I helped my uncle prepare a slow match of wet powder encased in linen.

By midnight the charge was rammed into the hole. The slow match uncoiled along the gallery and showed its end outside the opening. Only a spark was needed to ignite our fuse.

"Tomorrow," said my uncle.

I had to wait six long hours.

CHAPTER 19
The Great Explosion

I remember the next day very clearly. It never returns to my mind without a shudder of horror and my heart pounding. We were hurled along like the playthings of the fierce elements of the deep.

The moment drew near to clear a way by blasting through the opposing granite boulder. I begged for the honor of lighting the fuse. We calculated the fuse would burn for ten minutes before setting fire to the mine. I therefore had sufficient time to get away to the raft.

I took hold of the end of the match. My uncle stood, chronometer in hand. "Ready?" he cried.

"Yes!"

"Fire!"

I instantly plunged the end of the fuse into the lantern. It spluttered and flamed, and I ran quickly to the raft.

"Come on board quickly and let us push off," my uncle said.

Hans, with a vigorous thrust, sent us from the shore. The raft shot twenty fathoms out to sea. It was a moment of intense excitement. My uncle was watching the hand of the chronometer.

"Five more minutes!" he said. "Four! Three!"

My pulse was beating very quickly.

"Two! One! Down, granite rocks! Down with you!" my uncle cried.

What took place at that moment? I believe I did not hear the dull roar of the explosion. But the rocks suddenly assumed a new arrangement. I saw a bottomless pit open on the shore. The sea, lashed into sudden fury, rose up in an enormous billow. Our unhappy raft was lifted in the air with all its crew and cargo!

We all three fell down flat. In less than a second it became completely dark. Then I felt as if the raft had no support beneath it. I thought it was sinking, but it was not. I wanted to speak to my uncle, but the roaring of the waves prevented him from hearing me. I then understood what had taken place.

On the other side of the blown-up

rock was an abyss. The explosion had caused a kind of earthquake in this fissured region. A great gulf had opened, and the sea, now changed into a torrent, was hurrying us along into it. We were soon to be sucked into that abyss!

We held on to the raft for hours. We felt violent shocks whenever we crashed against the jagged rocks. Yet these shocks were not very frequent. So I concluded that the gully was widening. It was no doubt the same road that

Saknussemm had taken. But instead of walking peaceably down it, as he had done, we were carrying a whole sea along with us.

To judge by the air, which was whistling past me and making a whizzing sound in my ears, we were moving faster than the fastest trains.

Somehow, Hans did manage to light a lantern. We clung to the stump of the mast, which had snapped at the first shock of our great catastrophe. Of our instruments, none were saved but the compass and the chronometer. We had only one day's worth of food left!

I stupidly stared at our failing supplies. I refused to face the greatness of our loss. Even if we had enough food for months, it wouldn't help us get out of the abyss into which we were being hurled. Why should we fear the horrors of famine when death was facing us in many other forms?

I wondered grimly what our chances

were and decided not to share my thoughts with my uncle. I had the courage to keep silent. I wished to leave him cool and confident.

At that moment the light from our lantern burned itself out. Then, like a child, I closed my eyes firmly so I wouldn't have to face the darkness.

Our speed doubled. I could tell by the sharpness of the currents that blew past my face. The descent became steeper. I had an impression that we were dropping vertically. My uncle's hand, and the vigorous arm of Hans, held me fast.

Suddenly, after a space of time that I could not measure, I felt a shock. The raft had not struck against any hard resistance but had suddenly been stopped in its fall. A waterspout, an immense liquid column, was beating upon the surface of the waters. I was suffocating! I was drowning!

But this sudden flood was not of long duration. In a few seconds I found myself in the air again, which I inhaled with all the force of my lungs. My uncle and Hans were still holding me by the arms. And the raft was still carrying us.

CHAPTER 20
Speeding Upward Through the Horrors of Darkness

My hearing suddenly returned. I heard my uncle saying, "We are going up."

"What do you mean?" I cried.

"We are going up!" he pointed.

I stretched out my arm. I touched the wall and drew back a bleeding hand. We were ascending quickly.

"The torch!" my uncle cried.

Hans lit the torch. It provided enough light to show us what kind of a place we were in.

"Just as I thought," my uncle said. "We are in a tunnel. The water has reached the bottom of the gulf. It is now rising to its level and carrying us with it."

"Where to?" I asked.

"I don't know. But we must be ready for anything. We are rising at a speed of about ten miles per hour," he said.

"Yes, if nothing stops us and there is an opening. But what if there isn't?" I asked with concern. "If the air is condensed by the pressure of this column of water, we shall be crushed."

"Alex," replied my uncle with perfect coolness, "our situation is almost hopeless, but there are some chances

of survival. Let us then be prepared to seize upon the smallest advantage."

"But what shall we do now?" I asked.

"Keep our strength by eating," was his answer.

At these words I fixed a sad eye upon my uncle. "Eat, did you say?" I asked.

"Yes, at once," he replied.

My uncle added a few words in Danish, but Hans shook his head mournfully.

"What?" cried my uncle. "Have we lost our food?"

"Yes. Here is all we have left for the three of us," I said.

An hour passed. I began to feel the pangs of a violent hunger. My companions were suffering, too. Not one of us dared touch the wretched remnant of our food.

But we were now moving up with excessive speed. Sometimes the air would cut our breath short. The heat was increasing to cause the most fearful anxiety. The temperature was 100°F.

What could be the meaning of such a change? The theory of a central fire remained, in my opinion, the only one that was true. Were we heading to where the phenomena of central heat ruled and would reduce everything to the state of molten liquid? I feared this would be true.

"If we are neither drowned, nor shattered to pieces, nor starved to death, there is still the chance that we may be burned alive and reduced to ashes," I said.

My uncle shrugged his shoulders and returned to his thoughts.

Another hour passed. Except for a slight increase in the temperature, nothing new had happened.

"We must save our strength for the moment when we need it," my uncle said. "We should not let ourselves be weakened by hunger."

My uncle took the piece of meat and the few biscuits that had escaped destruction. He divided them into three equal portions and gave one to each. This made about a pound of food for each of us.

As soon as the meal was done, we each fell deep into thought. I could hear my uncle murmuring geological terms. I could understand them, and in spite of myself, I felt interested in this last geological study.

"Eruptive granite," he was saying. "We are still in the primitive period. But we are going up, up, higher still. Who can tell?"

He was examining the perpendicular wall. In a few minutes, he continued: "This is gneiss! Here is mica schist! Ah! Presently we shall come to the transition period, and then—"

What did my uncle mean? Could he be trying to measure the thickness of the crust of the earth that lay between us and the world above? Had he any means of making this calculation? No,

he did not have the aneroid, and no guessing could replace it.

Still, the temperature continued to rise and I felt myself steeped in a broiling atmosphere. Gradually, we had to remove our coats. The lightest covering became uncomfortable and even painful.

"Are we rising into a fiery furnace?" I asked. The heat was doubling.

"No," my uncle replied, "that is impossible!"

"Yet," I answered, feeling the wall, "this wall is burning hot."

At the same moment, touching the water, I had to withdraw my hand in haste.

"The water is scalding," I cried.

Then, an unconquerable terror seized me. I felt that a catastrophe was coming. A dim, vague notion came to my mind. By the flickering light of the torch I could see contortions in the granite beds. A phenomenon was unfolding in which electricity would play the principal part, then this unbearable heat, this boiling water! I consulted the compass.

The compass had lost its properties! The needle flew from pole to pole with a kind of frenzied impulse. It was broken!

CHAPTER 21
Shot Out of a Volcano!

According to the most modern theories, the mineral covering of the earth was always changing. Knowing this, a phenomenon of this kind would not have greatly alarmed me.

But other peculiar facts began to concern me. Continuous explosions and the compass being thrown out of gear by electrical currents confirmed a growing fear. The mineral crust of the globe threatened to burst. The granite foundations would come together with a crash. The fissure through which we were helplessly driven would be filled up. The void would be full of crushed fragments of

rock, and we would be buried!

"Uncle," I cried, "we are lost now, utterly lost!"

"What are you in a fright about now?" was the calm response. "What is the matter with you?"

"The matter? Look at those quaking walls! Look at those shaking rocks. Don't you feel the burning heat? Don't you see how the water boils and bubbles? Are you blind to the dense vapors and steam growing thicker and denser every minute? See this agitated compass needle? It is an earthquake that is threatening us," I cried.

"I think you are mistaken," my uncle said.

"What! Don't you recognize the signs?" I asked.

"Of an earthquake? No! I am looking out for something better," he replied.

"What can you mean? Explain," I said.

"It is an eruption," he said.

"An eruption! Do you mean that we are running up the shaft of a volcano?"

I asked.

"I believe we are," my uncle said. "And it is the best thing that could possibly happen to us under our circumstances."

"What?" I shouted. "Our fate has flung us here among burning lavas, molten rocks, boiling waters, and all kinds of volcanic matter. We are going to be pitched out, tossed up, spit out high into the air, along with fragments of rock and showers of ashes. And it is the best thing that could happen to us?"

"Yes," my uncle replied, "I don't see any other way of reaching the surface of the earth."

My uncle was right. Never had he seemed to me more daring in his notions than at this moment when he was calmly contemplating the chances of being shot out of a volcano!

In the meantime, up we went. The night passed away in continual ascent. The uproar around us became more intensified. It was evident that we were

being hurried upward upon the crest of a wave of eruption. Beneath our raft were boiling waters, and under these the more sluggish lava worked its way up in a heated mass. But, instead of ascending Snaefell, an extinct volcano, we were inside one in full activity. I wondered, therefore, where in the world we were.

Toward morning, the upward movement became faster. An enormous force drove us from below.

Soon, lights began to penetrate the vertical gallery, which widened as we went up. Right and left I could see deep channels, like huge tunnels, out of which escaped dense volumes of smoke. Tongues of fire lapped the walls, which crackled and sputtered under the intense heat.

"Those are only sulfurous flames and vapors, which one must expect to see in an eruption. They are quite natural," my

uncle said calmly. "They won't overcome us, since the gallery is widening. If it becomes necessary, we'll abandon the raft and creep into a crevice."

The heat was becoming unbearable. The perspiration streamed from my body. But for the speed of our ascent, we would have been suffocated.

My uncle gave up on abandoning the raft, since its planks gave us a firmer support against the elements. Then, at about eight in the morning, a new incident occurred. The upward movement ceased. The raft lay motionless.

"Has the eruption stopped?" I asked.

"I hope not," my uncle replied.

I rose and tried to look around me. Perhaps the raft itself, stopped in its course by a projection, was stopping the volcanic torrent. If this was the case, we would have to release it as soon as possible.

But it was not so. The blast of ashes and rubbish had ceased to rise.

"Ah!" my uncle said between his clenched teeth. "You are afraid. But don't alarm yourself—this lull cannot last long. It has lasted now five minutes, and in a short time we shall resume our journey to the mouth of the crater."

As he spoke, my uncle continued to consult his chronometer. He was again right. The raft was soon hurried and driven forward with a rapid but irregular movement. It lasted about ten minutes and then stopped again.

"In ten more minutes we shall be off again, for our present business lies with an intermittent volcano. It gives us time now and then to take a breath," my uncle said.

This was perfectly true. When the ten minutes were over, we started off again with renewed and increased speed. We had to hold the planks of the raft, so as not to be thrown off. It seemed evident that we were not in the main shaft of the volcano but in a lateral gallery

where this activity is common.

If it weren't for Hans, I would have more than once broken my head against the granite roof of our burning dungeon. I have no exact recollection of what took place during the following hours. Explosions, loud detonations and a general shaking of the rocks continued all around us. At one point our raft began to helplessly spin and whirl.

Snorting flames darted their fiery tongues at us. There were wild, fierce puffs of stormy wind from below. I could see Hans by the light of our torch just at the moment when I thought our journey had come to an inevitable and disastrous end.

CHAPTER 22
Sunny Lands in the Blue Mediterranean

Hans supported me with one arm and my uncle with the other. I was not seriously hurt, but I was shaken and bruised all over. I found myself lying on the sloping side of a mountain only two yards from a gaping chasm. Hans had saved me from death while I laid rolling dangerously close to the edge.

"Where are we?" I asked my uncle. "Is it Iceland?"

"No," Hans replied.

"What? Not Iceland?" my uncle cried.

This was our final surprise after all of the astonishing events of our wonderful journey. I expected to see a white cone covered with eternal snow rising from the midst of the barren deserts of the icy north. But we were sitting halfway down a mountain baked under the burning rays of a southern sun. We were getting blistered from the heat.

I could not believe my own eyes. But the heat and the sensation of burning left me no room for doubt. We had come out of the crater half-naked, and the sun to which we had been strangers for two months was now washing over us.

When my eyes grew accustomed to the bright light, I tried to figure out where we were.

My uncle was the first to speak. "Well, this is not much like Iceland. This is no northern mountain. There are no granite peaks capped with snow. Look!"

Above our heads, at a height of five hundred feet or more, we saw the crater of a volcano. At intervals of fifteen minutes or so there came loud explosions. There were also columns of fire, mingled with pumice stones, ashes and flowing lava. I could feel the heaving of the mountain. But at the mountain's base the earth was rich and green. I could see olives, figs and grape-covered vines. Beyond all this was a wide, blue expanse of sea or lake, which appeared to enclose this enchanting island. Eastward was a seaport village, and in the harbor a few vessels on the softly swelling waves. What a lovely sight after being in the darkness for so long.

"Where are we?" I asked faintly.

Hans closed his eyes with lazy indifference. My uncle looked around with dumb surprise. "Well, whatever mountain this may be," he said at last, "it is very hot here. The explosions are still going on. Let us get down to safety and find something to eat and drink."

"We are in Asia," I guessed. "We're on the coasts of India, in the Malay Islands, or in Oceania. We have passed through half the globe."

"But the compass?," my uncle said.

"Oh, the compass!" I said, greatly puzzled. "According to the compass, we have gone northward."

"Could it be wrong?" my uncle asked.

Here was something that baffled us completely. I did not know what to say.

We were coming into that delightful greenery, and began eating grapes by the mouthful. Not far off, under the delicious shade of the trees, I discovered a spring of fresh, cool water, in which we bathed our faces, hands and feet luxuriously.

While we relaxed, a child appeared out of a grove of olive trees.

"Here is an inhabitant of this happy land!" I cried.

It was but a poor boy. We frightened him with our ragged hair and torn clothes.

Just as the poor little wretch was going to run away, Hans caught him and brought him to us. My uncle asked him in German where we were. The child didn't answer.

"Very well," my uncle said. "I infer that we are not in Germany."

He asked the same question in English, then in French. The child was still silent.

"Now let us try Italian," my uncle said. *"Dove noi siamo?"*

"Yes, where are we?" I impatiently repeated.

But there was still no answer.

"Will you speak when you are told?" my uncle exclaimed. *"Come si noma questa isola?"*

"Stromboli," replied the little herd boy, slipping out of Hans's hands and running away at last.

Stromboli! We were in the midst of the Mediterranean Sea. And the distant blue mountains in the east were the mountains of Calabria. The threatening volcano far away to the south was the fierce Etna.

Having entered by one volcano, we

had come out of another more than two thousand miles from Snaefell and from that barren, far-away Iceland! The strange chances of our expedition had carried us into the heart of the fairest region in the world. We had left the murky sky and cold fogs of the frigid zone to revel under the blue sky of Italy!

We set off again to reach the port of Stromboli. We didn't want to startle the natives with our true story, so we presented ourselves as shipwrecked mariners.

On my way I could hear my uncle murmuring, "But the compass! That compass! It pointed due north. How are we to explain that fact?"

"My opinion is," I replied disdainfully, "that it is best not to explain it. That is the easiest way to shelve the difficulty."

"Indeed! A scientist of my level unable to explain the cause of a cosmical phenomenon! Why, it would be simply disgraceful!" And as he spoke, my uncle, half-dressed in rags, was himself again. He was learned and imposing, the stern German professor of mineralogy.

We arrived at the little port of San Vicenzo, where Hans claimed his wages for thirteen weeks' work, which was counted out to him with a hearty shaking of hands all around.

At that moment, he showed an emotion very unusual for him. I believe he smiled.

CHAPTER 23
All's Well That Ends Well

Such is the conclusion of a history that I cannot expect everybody to believe. For some people will believe nothing unless they experience it themselves.

After a few days of rest, we embarked on the steamer *Volturno*. In three days we were at Marseilles. We had nothing on our minds but that compass, which had now been misplaced. A few days later, in the evening, we arrived at Hamburg.

I cannot describe to you the astonishment of Martha or the joy of Gretchen.

"Now you are a hero, Alex," Gretchen said. "You will not leave me again!"

I looked tenderly at her, and she

smiled through her tears.

How can I describe the extraordinary sensation produced by the return of Professor Liedenbrock? Thanks to Martha's tattling, the news that my uncle had gone to discover a way to the center of the earth had spread over the world. People refused to believe it. Yet, the appearance of Hans tended to shake the confidence of the doubters.

Hamburg gave a grand party in our honor. My uncle related all about our expedition, with only one omission: the unexplained behavior of our compass. He donated the now famous document by Saknussemm to the archives of the city.

So much honor and fame excited more than envy. Since my uncle's questions of the theory of earth's central fire now rested upon observed fact, the current systems of science had to be reevaluated.

My uncle was saddened that our faithful Hans had decided to leave

Hamburg. We wanted him to stay. He was the man to whom we owed all our success and our lives, too. He would not let us reward him as we wished to do. He was homesick.

To conclude, I have to add that the account of this journey into the center of the earth created a sensation around the world. It was translated into many languages. Everyone discussed it. My uncle enjoyed the glory he had deservedly won.

One day, while arranging a collection of minerals in his cabinet, I noticed the compass, which we had long lost sight of. I opened it and began to watch it.

Suddenly, to my astonishment, I noticed a strange fact, and I uttered a cry of surprise.

"What is the matter?" my uncle asked.

"See, its poles are reversed!"

My uncle looked excitedly at it. "See there," he cried, as soon as he was able to speak. "After our arrival at Cape

Saknussemm, the north pole of the needle began to point south instead of
north."

"During the electric storm on the
Liedenbrock Sea, that ball of fire, which
magnetized all the iron on board,
reversed the poles of our magnet!"

"Aha! Aha!" shouted my uncle with a
loud laugh. "So it was just an electric
joke!"

From that day on, my uncle was the

most glorious of geniuses. And I was the happiest of men, for my pretty Gretchen took her position in the old house on the Konigstrasse in the double capacity of niece to my uncle and wife to a certain happy youth.

From then on, the illustrious Professor Otto Liedenbrock, corresponding member of all the scientific, geographical, and mineralogical societies of all the civilized world, was her uncle and mine.

About the Author

Jules Verne was born in 1828 in Nantes, France. His father was a very successful lawyer, and his mother came from a family of shipbuilders and sea captains.

In 1850, Verne's one-act comedy, *The Broken Straws*, was performed in Paris. Soon, Verne grew to love science and geography, although he had no formal training in either field.

Throughout his life, Verne wrote sixty-five novels, more than twenty short stories and essays, and thirty plays. His most famous works include *Journey to the Center of the Earth*, *20,000 Leagues Under the Sea*, and *Around the World in Eighty Days*.

Jules Verne died in 1905 at the age of seventy-seven in Amiens, France. His works developed the foundation of modern science fiction.

Treasury of Illustrated Classics

Adventures of Huckleberry Finn
The Adventures of Pinocchio
The Adventures of Robin Hood
The Adventures of Sherlock Holmes
The Adventures of Tom Sawyer
Alice in Wonderland
Anne of Green Gables
Beauty and the Beast
Black Beauty
The Call of the Wild
Frankenstein
Great Expectations
Gulliver's Travels
Heidi
Jane Eyre
Journey to the Center of the Earth
The Jungle Book
King Arthur and the Knights of the Round Table
The Legend of Sleepy Hollow & Rip Van Winkle
A Little Princess
Little Women
Moby Dick
Oliver Twist
Peter Pan
The Prince and the Pauper
Pygmalion
Rebecca of Sunnybrook Farm
Robinson Crusoe
The Secret Garden
Swiss Family Robinson
The Time Machine
Treasure Island
20,000 Leagues Under the Sea
White Fang
The Wind in the Willows
The Wizard of Oz